For James, who made the sand giant
—(J.D)

For Sally
—(M.E.)

First American edition published 1999 by
Crocodile Books, USA
An imprint of Interlink Publishing Group, Inc.
99 Seventh Avenue • Brooklyn, New York 11215 and
46 Crosby Street • Northampton, Massachusetts 01060

Text copyright © 1999 Joyce Dunbar
Illustrations copyright © 1999 Mark Edwards

Published simultaneously in Great Britain by
Macdonald Young Books
an imprint of Wayland Publishers Ltd

Library of Congress Cataloging-in-Publication Data
Dunbar, Joyce
    The Sand Children / Joyce Dunbar; illustrated by Mark Edwards
      p. cm.
    Summary : A boy and his father make a sand giant while camping at the
beach, and during the night it comes to life to make sand children.
    ISBN 1-56656-309-7
    [1. Beaches—Fiction. 2. Giants—Fiction.] I. Edwards, Mark, ill.
II. Title
PZ7.D8944San 1999
[E]—dc21   98-46852
                                               CIP
                                             AC

Printed and bound in Belgium

For a complete catalog of
Crocodile illustrated children's books,
please write to us at the above address
or call us toll-free at
1-800-238-LINK

The Sand Children

JOYCE DUNBAR

Illustrated by

Mark Edwards

Crocodile Books, USA

An imprint of Interlink Publishing Group, Inc.
NEW YORK

When Dad took me camping on the beach, I made a line of sand castles. Then Dad helped me to make a sand giant. We made his hair with dried seaweed and shaped his teeth like little sand turrets. We used a cockleshell for his belly button and mussel shells for his deep blue eyes. We gave him big fat fingers and toes.

I sat down by his side. I leaned on his great round belly and grinned at his great big grin. We both sat staring out to sea.

When it began to get dark, Dad said it was time to go back and have some supper.

"But I don't want to leave my sand giant," I said. "The sea will come and wash him away."

"Perhaps the tide won't come in this far," said Dad.

So we said good-bye to the sand giant and went back to our tent on the dunes. I could still see the sand giant. He had the whole wide beach to himself.

"Won't he be lonely?" I said.
But as I watched, some children came along the shore.
They were running and shouting and laughing.

When they got to my line
of sand castles, they trampled
them one by one.
"They'll trample the sand
giant!" I said. "We must run
and stop them!"
"We're too far away," said
my dad. "They might leave
him alone. Watch."

So we knelt down and watched from the dunes. The children went up to the sand giant and slowly walked round and round him.

"They might kick him!" I said, but they didn't. They stared into his face and pointed.

"They might poke his eyes out!" I said, but they didn't. They talked to him and tickled his toes.

"They might knock his head off," I said, but they didn't. They jumped and danced about between his arms and legs.
"They like him," I said. And they did. They patted and hugged and stroked him. Then they waved good-bye.
"He liked them, too," said my dad. "Now it's time for some sleep. He might still be there in the morning."

That night the moon shone into our tent. I woke up and peeped outside. The sand giant was no longer sitting down. He was busy with his great big hands, making things in the sand. He waved, and I waved back. He wanted me to join him.

I crept out of the tent and scrambled over the dunes.
What was the sand giant making? Children—children in
the sand. But the sand children had no faces.

"Shall I give them faces?" I asked.
The sand giant grinned and nodded. I liked the face I had given him.

As soon as I gave them faces, the
sand children came to life. Soon
there were seven sand children.
We ran and laughed and played.
Then together we made a sand castle
with a hall and magnificent rooms.
We ate at a driftwood table, and
I went to sleep in a driftwood bed.
I felt it drifting away. . .

But in the morning I woke up
in the tent.
I went rushing to see the sand
giant. He was sitting just where
we'd made him, with his big
fat fingers and toes.
But there wasn't a sign of the
sand children. Except . . .

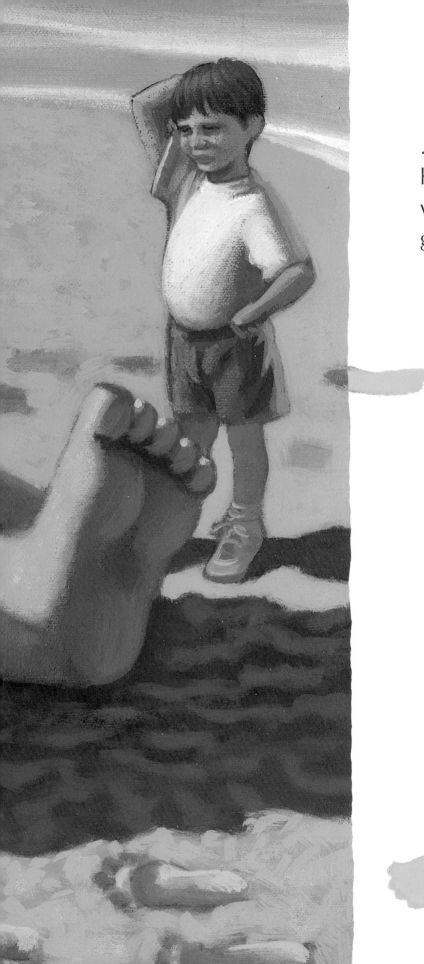

. . . footprints all around him in the sand. And where had the sand castle gone?

I told Dad all about the
sand children and the
castle where we played.
"You must have been
dreaming," he said.
"I wasn't, was I?"
I whispered to the sand giant.
"You remember, don't you?"
A mussel shell fell from
his face.
And I *know* that he winked!